"Skid Row"

Dyl Elner

I

Welcome to hell, I'm the devil. This is my dominion; a run-down neighborhood in Prague, full of drunks, whores, thieves and lawyers. Aside from my many malevolent names, I'll just stick with Franz, although I find Lucifer more appealing. A while back, I used to be one of the best damn violinists in Bohemia (go figure), then I quit. I don't know why, but I just kicked it and moved from a nice flat in Prague to a dingy flat in Skid Row. Not too far from town, but far enough below Limbo and across the river Styx.

I still have my instrument, a genuine Stradivarius. The man who gave it to me must be rolling in his grave to know that a sleaze like me still has it. Lately I don't have any desire to even touch my violin. I almost forget it's even under my bed, hell, for all I know it could have been stolen and the thief could be living in Monte Carlo with the money he made off of it. But who am I kidding? Nobody in Skid Row can tell a Stradivarius from a toy fiddle, I'll bet half the people who live here have ever heard the word Stradivarius.

Life in this world is always the same dismal routine; I wake up at ten or eleven, stare at the crumbling plaster on the ceiling, listening to what I call 'The Radio.' This being the loud conversations from my next-door neighbors. Last week, the program ended with the lady being shoved against the wall by her husband as he stormed out, leaving her to weep bitterly. Odd as this sounds, I find something aesthetic in a woman's sorrow, like the music of Wagner sans libretto. Once I finally decide to get off my dead ass, I shit and shave, re-grease my hair, and start the day with some instant coffee, black with a shot of whiskey. I brood over my cup for a while, usually in the Summer I wait until high noon is over before I go out.

Lately I don't really do anything these days. When I moved here I used to play on the streets and in the metro but I got tired of the fame. I can't stand people, but at the same time I don't mind company that leaves me alone. In my small circle of friends, there's my landlady, Ms. Krovar, or Inga as she prefers I call her. She often has me come over for tea or supper, or sometimes just to listen to her collection of opera records. She's the only person I know who really understands music, unlike every uptight philistine who call themselves music lovers. The worst were the conductors; overpaid clowns who can read music and wag a little stick.

On one occasion after finishing a bottle of cheap port, she got me into bed. Out of every woman I've courted, I'll be fair and rate her a nine out of ten. It seems like the occasional fuck keeps me from killing myself, but why would I even bother? Where am I going to go, hell? It's too late, I'm already there. Instead of little gremlins and burning sulfur pits, it's full of drunks, whores, pimps, thieves and heroin. Its black and grey, with dilapidated roads and buildings, shadowed by an abandoned brewery the size of a cathedral. Also, it's always cold, even in summer.

Other types I encounter include the town drunk, Boris. He's basically Santa Claus in a tattered brown coat and a driver's cap. But he's still jolly, fat and has a bushy, white, dandruff-ridden beard. He always smells of peppermint schnapps, and if I don't see him passed out in the gutter with a smile on his face, he's always at the pub, cheering us up with a night of singing and crude jokes. I can listen to the same joke from Boris twice and still laugh. Despite being a slob, the ladies love the man, I always see some of the local women gathered around his table, sometimes taking him home or to the hotel where he lives. I think he may as well be the only happy man in the world. Everyone else here in Skid Row is a soul-sucking vampire.

Take another friend of mine, Vaclav, the town philosopher. Like any intellectual, I always see him brooding over a glass of scotch, rambling on about everything from morality to political theory. I can't take a damn thing he says seriously. According to him, we as Europeans are all born into privilege, thus making us morally bankrupt compared to people of less well-to-do nations. Rightfully, we the privileged few should give all of our money, property and faith to the state and share it for the good of the underclass. The man venerates Karl

Marx as if he where Jesus Christ, and at the same time calls Nietzsche the devil. I can tell without question he's a Communist, all though he's too lazy to be an active one. The last time I bought it up he yelled at me and made a big scene at the bar. I was too drunk to remember the details, but according to the bartender, he tried to punch me and I knocked him over with a blow to the gut. He left crying like a little bitch. Despite what happened, we shook on it (by shake I mean drink), and eventually things went back to normal. He was the same pessimistic, self-indulgent goon I knew.

Lastly, when I go for a walk in the evening, I usually go to the public park where I always find the cigarette girl. A little tomboy, who always makes a route around town with a trey full of cigarettes, sometimes she has a little reefer hidden in there. Also, she always sings the Russian song Korobushka. I like her a lot, she'd make a good jazz singer, and she always keeps me stocked up on smokes, and when I want company that isn't drunk or loose, she's always a better option. There are other less important types in town; there's Moshe the Jew, a thief and hustler whom I can't help but notice has an eye on the cigarette girl, Dolf the pimp, and his enemy Natasha the courtesan. She's basically a one-woman escort service, too independent for a pimp. From what I know, she makes better money than Dolf. It's no secret that the pimp is also the enforcer of Moshe's law, at least when the town constable is too drunk to keep the law of the land in check.

There are also other people of interest in this town; aside from crooks outside the law there are crooks who went to school for it. There's the shyster lawyer who occupies the office near Moshe's pawnshop, and there's the three town doctors, who occupy the clinic not too far from the pub district.

It's not uncommon for people to seek medical attention here in Skid Row, at least those that don't choose to drop like flies indiscriminately. In fact, some people value their lives well enough to stay significantly healthy, and the three doctors serve that purpose, no insurance required. The oldest is Doctor Rubenstein, the physician, who in his heyday was one of the most celebrated proctologists in Prague. Rumor has it that he was the personal physician for the Duke of Sweden who suffered from terrible IBS. But times changed, and sticking his hand up diseased sphincters exclusively was too much for the old man, so he went back to med school and became a regular physician, and saw it as his Christian duty to serve the underclass. That being said, he set up shop in Skid Row and now he's stuck here. Not that he really cares, the man loves his work so much he doesn't know how miserable he really is.

The second doctor is the town Dentist, Doctor Suliz. A few years younger than Rubenstein but just as old and haggard. When he isn't wrist deep in somebody's mouth, he's always shaking, no thanks to rubbing cocaine tooth-powder in his gums like its candy. The third is by far the creepiest, and probably the most perverse of the three doctors, is Doctor Klas, the town podiatrist. He's the youngest of the doctors and instead of having a bushy beard like his colleagues, is clean shaven save the pencil thin moustache, and he's also bald. His office is by far the most mediaeval, and that's saying a lot compared to the dentist's office. Hell, Rubenstein's office has an electroshock therapy machine in a cabinet by his operating chair.

Doctor Kass's office is decked with anatomical models and pictures of feet, including a skeleton foot which he keeps on the shelf nearest his desk. I've had the displeasure of needing his service once; while out drinking, I impaled my foot on a nail and he removed it. The man asked if he could keep my holey sock as a token, since he had a box full of famous people's socks which he believed where holy relics. These included the lost socks of everyone from Napoleon, to Beethoven, to Catherine the Great, all of which he paid a few thousand gulden a pair.

There you have it, this is my dominion of the damned, Skid Row, the one part of Earth eternally hidden from God. I could bore you with more details about it, as if I were the infernal tour guide, but here's a more interesting story that happened recently. As usual, I got up at noon, woken by my landlady vacuuming her floor. It was unusually sunny out, and the blinding light caused be to roll over and fall on my face. After grunting my choicest obscenities, I dragged myself into the kitchen, still in my boxers, and put the kettle on. Since I showered last night, I quickly dressed and greased my hair. That being done, I went to see if The Radio was on.

And I was right, just as I put a shot of bourbon in my cup of coffee, the couple next door where at it again. I chuckled as the man whined and bitched about how he was too lame to get a job while the woman emasculated him. Things began to become inaudible when I heard someone pounding at their door. The landlady seemed to have had enough of their fighting and decided to get involved. Knocking back the last of my coffee, I took this chance to slip out of the building and walked down the street. The sunshine that woke me up was gone within seconds. Skid Row was the same as always, dark and damask. Children were running barefoot in the streets and the welfare queens were on the porch, all of whom had a baby or two in their arms. Some of the children were dancing around a woman passed out with a needle in her arm.

Other street children were throwing rocks at an abandoned building, each trying to break a window or knock down a door. One of them managed to shatter a window on the ground floor, and they all cheered as they all climbed into the black space, some coming out with handfuls of stolen goods; jewels, spoiled food, strips of carpet, planks of wood and anything they could get their hands on, some just went in to tear the place up.

Shops and bars where still open, the grocer was stacking fruit on his cart and shouting at bums who tried to steal his stock. The barber, however, was boarding up his own store, crying knowing he was out of business. Every other shop in the district was either boarded up or barely making it, yet the liquor store and the Moshe's Pawnshop were open, doing good business as usual. The man was behind his counter examining a sack of gold coins which he stacked neatly to one side, despite being open 12 hours a day, the door was always locked and

Moshe kept a loaded shotgun in plain sight behind a counter. No thieves could steal from this thief and go home alive. One poor soul actually never left the store at all. Once Moshe caught him in the act, he blew the man's head to kingdom come and dissolved the body in lye. He then dumped the soupy remains in the sewer in broad daylight, this served as a warning to the locals never to try crossing him. Yet other lowlifes made their own living without getting caught. Burglars, pickpockets, peddlers and the lawyers around here kept to their business and rarely feuded.

When any kind of feud broke out it was bloodier than a western thriller. Hell, sometimes it was as if the Germans invaded again, only it was a fight among low lives and people with no criminal inklings would die in the crossfire. Sometimes a feud would break out over the pettiest reason; a bad drug deal, a boy getting the clap from a whore, undercooked spaghetti, a dirty beer glass, you name it.

That's one of the reasons I shelved my violin, these petty turf wars were scaring off my customers and the last thing

I needed was some scumbag stealing my money or killing me for it. That's when I started carrying my father's pistol with me everywhere I went, even just when I went to the corner store to buy the newspaper. However, I stopped carrying it after a month, seeing that there were no feuds going on for some time.

Coming across the old brewery, I heard a high baritone voice singing 'O du liber Augustin' loud enough to echo in the dilapidated building. Obviously, this was Boris, nobody in this neighborhood sings that song, at least not as merrily as Boris. Amused, I put my hands in my pockets and leaned against the wall, listening to every verse, occasionally interrupted by a belch or hiccup. I was about to go into the brewery and join the man, but my mood was altered by the sight of a man in a duster coat, biting his nails as he shuffled toward me. I knew all too well what this man wanted, he was just another junkie looking for a fix, and was desperate enough to beg for it. Joke was on him, I had nothing to give! I left the flat that morning without my wallet.

Without much talk, the junkie just sauntered away. He must have known I had nothing, like himself. The smarter junkies in town have a sixth-sense when it comes to pocket change, and every pick-pocket uses it to their advantage. When you're addicted to heroin, you don't give a damn who you steal from, as long as you get a few gulden towards your next hit, you're in business.

The more refined types in Skid Row prefer to smoke opium, while the rest of the vermin around here shoot up. Some go as far as to stick it in the veins of their thumbs, between the toes, the jugular, and in their dicks if they're that desperate. I've had the privilege of trying it with an old friend of mine, a local dandy who smoked it, snuffed it, and when he had the money for the purest dosage, he shot up. It was through him I became more complacent with my new life in Skid Row when I first moved in. No thanks to puffing from his hookah, I now transitioned from the rush of cocaine to the languid decadence of opium, thus my cares of being damned for all eternity were a thing of the past.

With the dandy on my side, and my new love for opium and cheap sex, there was no heartache, no remorse, and no need for my integrity as an artist. All that mattered was getting my next fix for the day and I was set for life. I always preferred to smoke it being terrified of needles, yet the dandy would stick those things in his veins like it didn't matter. He was very clever with this habit; being a tailor by trade, the dandy kept his loaded needles in elastic bands sewn inside his tailcoat, or in a special cigarette case if he wore a frock coat. He would even shoot up at the café table of the whorehouse the same way one lights up a smoke. Finally, one evening the dandy convinced me to stop pussyfooting around and shoot up, claiming the high was better.

That being said and done, the dandy and I went back to his garret where he prepared a needle and tourniquet for me. It stung a little but once he pushed the plunger I felt my soul leave my body. When I woke up, the party was over. The dandy was dead and I was the one who found his mangled body on the floor. Soon enough, an ambulance came and took him straight to the city morgue, where I was bombarded with questions by the doctors and a police officer. The dandy had little to no next of kin who cared about him, save a few former lovers glad to see him go. Because of the state of his body, it was determined that he be buried hastily in a closed coffin, and since he was a mitzvaed Jew, the town rabbi granted him his last rites. I even played the violin for him at his funeral, as he once requested. Nobody showed up at the funeral, to my surprise, not even anyone who wanted to dance on his grave as the dandy boasted about. Only the rabbi came, who said a few simple prayers in Czech and Hebrew and not much else.

Once the junkie was out of sight, I went into the brewery. Near an enormous vat that once brewed beer, Boris was laying against the brick wall, empty beer bottles scattered around the floor. All around, the rats and cockroaches stopped to listen to him, some drunk on the leftover beer. Some even paired up and danced. My spirits lifted, I started to sing along.

"Rock ist veg, stock ist veg,

Augustin liegt in dreck!

O du Liber Augustin, Alles ist Hin!"

"Aha! Herr Maestro Franz! You know this song?" Boris said, with a gay hiccup.

"Know it, I wrote it!" I said, smugly.

"Well, don't just stand there, man! Grab a pint and join me. Come, sit a spell, its four o'clock somewhere, sing with me and be merry while the Lord grants us good health!"

I didn't need to be told twice, so I went over to the stockpile of factory sealed beer and grabbed us a couple. Boris always carried a bottle-opener and a corkscrew in his pocket, so the drinks flowed freely. Between verses of O Du liber Augustin, we switched to other drinking songs that could be heard blocks away as if this old brewery were a proper beer hall, minus the band. But in my drunken stupor, the waltzing rats and cockroaches soon picked up their own instruments to play along, each with little tubas, trumpets, trombones, saxophones, accordions and one little hammer and anvil. At the height of my stupor, they began to play the Bohemian National Polka, the Feuerfest by Joseph Strauss.

The whirlwind of oomph music got to a point where my head started swimming. This was a classic case of the spins. I blacked out within seconds. After some time, I got up not knowing if I was going to puke, piss or shit. This was probably one of the worst hangovers I ever had in a decade. I stood up to get myself steady on my feet, trying to get the light back in my eyes but the orange haze wouldn't wear off, so I sat back down to rest my eyes for a while. The brewery was dead quiet, save the dripping of the leaking pipes and the scuttling rats. Something wasn't right. Normally when I do my drinking with Boris, he snores like a lion when he passes out.

I rubbed the haze out of my eyes and found out what was wrong with the picture. In the dim blue light from the broken skylight above, the brewery looked dead. The hoppy smell of pilsner beer now smelled of death and decay. Where the oomph bands once stood were piles of broken glass, puddles of blood and urine. The rats were feasting one the carcasses of the dead and in the stench of decay, flies hung around and where in turn eaten by big fat spiders who descended from the rafters above. To my left, a huge pack of rats where crawling over one another to get a taste of the rotting corpse. I now realized without a doubt that Boris was dead. He lay there getting eaten by the rats, his urine and vomit-soaked body drawing the hungry vermin en-masse.

The only happy man in the world was dead. It struck me that I would have to be the bearer of bad news to the town. Brushing myself off, I went outside where an old couple was sitting nearby, with a basket of bread and wine as if on a picnic. The old lady looked to me and said "Maestro, is the show over so soon?"

It didn't take long for the word to get out to all of Skid Row. This already dismal town suddenly became even more depressing than before, if that was possible. Although Boris was baptized a Catholic, no real funeral was held. However, the priest and the rabbi, both of whom where lovers as rumor had it, joined us at the pub as well as all of Boris's lovers who wore their black veils for the occasion. Many of these women went to the brewery to mourn. After only one beer with the fellows and plenty of unwanted attention, I went home. I smelled as if I hadn't bathed in weeks, so Ms. Krovar let me have a soak in her bathtub, mine leaked into the apartment below and it was only a matter of time before it collapsed. While I bathed, she made us dinner and opened a bottle of wine from her cabinet, afterward we sat in silence in her den, which we often did. Ms. Krovar was the perfect kind of company, and she was very attractive for her age, being in her early forties, this she credits to not having kids. She was silent when I had nothing to say and like a broken record when I did. However, the silence had to be broken, a local whom this whole town would miss died and what little happiness we all here had was gone.

"Franz, you shouldn't be too hard on yourself," she said. "You act as if you killed a man."

"Killed a man?" I said, "Boris was the one drinking stale, lukewarm beer, I only joined him."

"Oych, I'm surprised you don't have a tapeworm at this point, you know spoiled pork-chops killed Mozart! You ought to know better. But what's the use warning a meshugina like yourself, always drinking like a fountain, and you never play your violin anymore!"

"Of course, I do, if I don't sell it for beer money," I said. "And I've got plenty where that came from, so why bother?"

The landlady snorted sarcastically. "Yeesh, you're just as bad as my poor Murray, zay gezunt, the man could drink a shlub like you under the table. And you're just as careless with money as he was. Give me a break, a talented violinist such as yourself ought to care, yet you're wasting such a talent on nothing. You're an artist!"

"I was an artist."

"Well with that attitude, I guess you're a bum like everybody in this fekakhded building. Only difference is you pay your rent and keep me company, otherwise its out you go, Maestro!"

I had nothing to say, so I acknowledged her with silence, which she was used to. There was no arguing with her, anyway. Ms. Krovar took a big swig of her wine and decided to end the silence with some music. Since I wouldn't make any like old times, she went to her library of phonographs and took one out at random.

"Ah, Reiner Lipchitz, now there's a great violinist. Have you ever heard him, Franz? He seems up your alley."

"Heard him, I knew him. I even have his violin!" I said.

Ms. Krovar looked at me shocked. "You're pulling my leg!"

"No, I'm serious. I knew the man long before he died, he got me to where I was before, and I inherited his violin."

"But the man played a Stradivarius, who would give up such a fine instrument like that?"

"He gave it to me, and he wrote it in his will. Nobody else was up for it, not even his own students where worthy enough in his eyes. Hell, none of his family even played!"

Ms. Krovar stared at the album cover, which was a sepia photo of Lipchitz in his prime, playing his Strad with that cold, statuesque look on his face. That was, in his eyes how a real violinist should look; the audience wants to see a man play and sound good, and he can't sound good on the violin when he looks as if he's laughing or crying, the emotion must come from the music itself, not the musician. "You never told me any of this!" she said.

"Well, I didn't feel like it!" I retorted, shrugging. In fact, I only told her enough over the two years I've known Ms. Krovar; that I was a violinist, I had a few records sold in Prague alone, others I made when traveling in America. That I was a drunk, a playboy and recently got out of prison for drunken disorderly conduct, among other things. "What is he playing?"

"Mendelssohn." The landlady said, and with that she put on the record and sat back. For half an hour, we listened to the concerto played on the violin I would soon own years after that record was cut. During the adagio, I began to think deeply about my past, about how I would play this very piece so many times to a point where I could play it in my sleep. How I had a successful career that I now wasted, and it got to a point where I missed it all. During the third and final movement, I was sitting on the edge of my seat, thinking about all of the musicians I would rub shoulders with, especially my father, who was a conductor and pianist well known in his time, and whose name I would bear like a badge of honor. All of this came crashing down as I began to feel for the second, and last, time in my life hot tears flood my eyes. Suddenly I felt as if the icy feeling in my body thawed, like I had never felt warmth before.

The landlady looked at me perplexed and it felt shameful to look at her in this state. I hid my eyes from her as I tried to hide my sobs. "Maestro, you're weeping, don't hide it!"

"No I'm not, fuck!" I said choking up, I was shaking all over like an epileptic. Something in me was forcing its way out, but I was holding it in like a madman. Almost immediately I stopped crying on command.

"Christ, I need a cigarette." I said, reaching in my pocket. I found nothing. "Damn, all out!"

With that, I got up and excused myself, leaving the apartment to go get a pack of smokes.

II

Before I finish telling my story, I'm going to bore you with the story of my fall from grace. Like I said, when I was one of the best damn violinists in Bohemia I'm not lying.

I grew up in a musical family, but was the only one to go into music as a career and keep it. I was the youngest of three children. My brother, Klaus, played cello and my sister, Katya, played piano for a while but became a dancer. My mother played violin. By the time I was two, she got me playing the instrument. She was my first teacher until I was 6. She did try to get Klaus to play the violin at first, but he hated it, it was too high pitched. Mother suggested he try viola instead, but my father intervened; "Viola!" he shouted, laughing. "Get this man a cello, instead." With that, he took my brother to watch a cellist at work playing Bach and the lad fell in love with the instrument.

My father was the music-director in the family. He himself was a conductor and pianist. A native of Kiev, he moved to Prague and became a not just a Czech, but a patriotic Czech. His newfound citizenship was a second religion. He and my mother agreed that I should be named after the one composer they worshipped like a god, Franz Liszt.

In his heyday, my father was the most respected conductor in town. Because he liked to travel, he never accepted the post of music director of the Prague Philharmonic, no matter how many times the producers begged him. He was like a great rabbi of music, wise and cunning but also very worldly despite his strict Orthodox Christian upbringing. He was a disciple of Apollo and Bacchus. Though Russian born, he became a Czech when he met my mother, a Moravian of gypsy lineage, which passed on to me and my sister. Whereas we had dark hair and eyes, my father had silvery-blond hair which whitened as he aged, much like his idol, Liszt. Klaus became father's doppelganger later in life. Being financially stable from his work conducting, teaching and playing at the piano bar, retired at fifty to be a father, first and foremost.

When I was 12, they sent me and my siblings to be educated in Russia; my brother and I studied at the same school for music as my father, St Petersburg Conservatory. My sister studied at Vaganova Academy. While in the country, we lived with my grandmother and aunt at their estate near the city, where we had the company of a few cousins and friends who would regularly show up. My aunt was an opera singer in her youth but retired and joined the church choir. Overtime, not only did I learn from the masters who worked with my father to make him the musical magus he was, I did also pick up Russian as a second language. This I dropped in favor of English when I was older, so eventually I forgot Russian entirely over time.

I graduated top of my class as one of the more promising violinists. My teacher, who was a magician with the fiddle, insisted that I was not his student, but a student of God and Paganini. Thanks to him, I was recommended to study at

Prague Conservatory. After we came back to Prague for good, the violin was no longer just a plaything but my life's work. Father insisted I dedicate my time to study, but I aced my work without much effort. While I was a student, I became a somewhat of a boulevardier; when I wasn't practicing, shut away in a coffin with a piano in it, I would always hit the town sharply dressed, just living on the streets of Prague. People liked me due to the fact that I was studying music, it was a badge of honor second only to being in the military. I was an arrogant bastard, but it got me pretty far. Most nights the gents from Conservatory and I would hit the beer-hall or a room above the local pub. We'd drink, smoke cigars and discuss everything from the opera to the latest partner one of us had in bed.

When I was 21, I graduated and was playing in the Prague Philharmonic. Though I was one of the more promising violinists to audition, I was put in the back of the row of Second Violin. It wasn't the gig I really wanted, but it was enough to keep bread on the table. I was living in an attic apartment in Old Town, where I slept in a mattress on the floor and ate on an industrial spool which served as my dining table. Mother insisted on having dinner on that damn thing on my first Christmas away from home. Hey, it was the artist's life, and I wouldn't have had it any better! At the time, Klaus was teaching cello part-time while he studied mathematics. He was a genius with math while I was always a substandard calculator. Katya went on to become a ballerina.

Tragedy struck, cutting their musical lives short. After father died, Klaus dedicated himself to managing his financial affairs. Being the math-buff, he was, Klaus went on to become an accountant, though he often kept his cello in the corner of his office and played just to blow off steam. Katya suffered a broken ankle, which to a perfectionist like her, was more tragic than losing a leg. Sometime later, she quit the ballet and got married on impulse. I actually never saw her again. Mother was the one who was affected the most. She found my father lying unconscious on the floor, under the family Bosendorfer. Father was gravely ill. At the age of seventy, he had a stroke that paralyzed his left hand, and he became more like the god Saturn than Apollo. He became sluggish, ill-tempered, and so depressed he couldn't get out of his chair. Before his stroke, he would dance and do kart-wheels in the house, and he would do pull-ups like an ape on steroids. Now he was a shadow of the man he was before. He couldn't feed himself or even go to the toilet unaided, and to make matters worse he couldn't play the piano anymore, at least not as good as he used to. That's what devastated him the most, the one thing he was put on this planet to do was taken away from him. He died sitting at the piano, trying to play O du Liber Augustin. That song would annoy the shit out of mother whenever father sang it, but now it would traumatize her to hear it again, and it would go on to haunt me to this day.

While my family toiled in their music-deprived misery, my luck changed when I befriended the great virtuoso, Reiner Lipchitz. The man became a good friend and mentor, and helped me reach his level of greatness. In my first solo show, the two of us did Bach's Double Violin Concerto, and afterward I performed the Chaconne. The Chaconne, when played right, is a rite of passage for any violinist that defines him as an artist. Within weeks I was the toast of the music world. I was no longer the graduate chamber musician in the back row of the orchestra, but a soloist. My new job as a soloist got me even farther then I could imagine, and pretty soon I had the means to be the boulevardier I was before.

I worked to live and indulge. I was a bit of a libertine with the ladies, but that changed when I met the goddess in the flesh. My muse, Janina. She was not only beautiful with her almond skin and green eyes, but she had a hell of a voice when she sang. Janina was originally an opera singer in training but rebelled against her parents by becoming a jazz singer. Not only that, she could play the guitar like a demon. When we met in the club she sang at, she told me she had a soft spot for Schubert, and I used that to win her heart.

One evening, I surprised her with an impromptu concert. I waited outside her apartment window until I got her attention. She stood at her window in her robe, smoking her cigarette out of a long holder as she greeted me. I played for her Schubert's Serenade. That being done, she beckoned me to her room where we made love for the first time. She was mine forever, or so I thought.

When I was just about to turn 30, Lipchitz had a second stroke that put him on his death bed. Before he kicked it, he invited me to his home in Brno where what remained of his family had gathered, as if they were waiting for the man to die so they could get their grubby mitts on his money. Everybody wanted one thing, his Stradivarius. As it turned out, none of them could even play Twinkle-Twinkle Little Star, and I was the one who inherited the instrument. Not only did he present it to me in person, but it was written in his will.

The sheer fact that I had that instrument got me rubbing shoulders with the big names in music. I had the means to travel anywhere at will; Janina and I liked traveling to America the most. Greece was fine, but we always preferred the Caribbean. For the purpose of music, I always liked Chicago better than New York. Living among Chicagoans, I developed a taste for the blues. Thanks to the music director in Chicago, I would always get a few blues records sent by mail. Not only that, Janina and I would frequent the smoky blues bars in town where we heard some of the big names of jazz and blues music, Dizzy Gillespie, Louis Armstrong, Lead Belly, Blind Willie McTell, you name it.

However, living the artist's life had its downs more so than it had ups, and soon the good times began to go bad, and slowly. Looking back, this was the time when I was really at my peak, but I was obsessed with getting higher on the food chain, so much to a point where I took what few good times I had for granted. I had a successful career and a loving woman to share a life with, but I blew it. My downfall began as such; one day after a mediocre performance of the Dvorak Concerto, I spent weeks beating myself up over it, drinking myself to sleep at night. I refused to show up to rehearsals for a while, once I even lashed out at the conductor. The audience came expecting a show but instead were treated to a complete snore-fest. While I sawed away on the violin, the orchestra was coaxed into a harsh cacophony that made no lasting impression. The conductor beat and wagged his baton like a dictator giving a rally and the orchestra either played poorly under the pressure or slouched lazily in their chairs, giving the concerto no effort, at all.

I gave that concerto everything I had, and that jackass had the gall to treat Dvorak as if he were the same as Verdi. This conductor had a bit of a homosexual obsession with Verdi, hailing the composer as his lord and master. All other composers where subservient to Verdi in the conductor's eyes, even Bach. This conductor wasn't even a Czech or Slovak, he was a Sicilian immigrant who bought and slept his way to the top, in fact he had no ear for music. The fact that he had a wealthy uncle who paid half the orchestra's revenue got him a job as a guest conductor, and rumor had it he was aiming to take the place of the music director when he died.

It was bad enough that every concert this conductor gave was substandard, and every time I gave the orchestra an audience, I would leave dissatisfied. Not only was I bored, but the audience and orchestra was bored. Every musician would be dead of boredom, slouching in their chares while the Dego Conductor wagged his baton like a substandard magician doing invisible illusions. Soon enough, I got tired of this man's pompousness and spoke out, venting my frustration to anyone who would listen. Much to my surprise, my rambling got out and spread like wildfire. I was having the same influence of musical opinion my father, the great high priest of music. Whenever my father saw so much as a chink in the armor of a bad musician, he'd be quick to point it out. Some musicians benefited greatly from his critiques while others sank in a pool of their own making, refusing to do better to a point where they failed.

For the first time, I felt a likeness to my father, a war hero and a highly respected artist. Somehow, father had cast a shadow that I lived under as a youth, admiring and envious of his influence, but now I was becoming more like him, an acclaimed maestro, and bearing my father's surname was only the surface of my being. If I was to make my father proud, it was time to take action, to put myself in his shoes.

It was high time I put my foot down and give the orchestra the kick in the ass it needed. If I was going to be a disciple of Apollo, I needed to preach his gospel. I wanted to lobby with the orchestra to have that Sicilian bastard banned from Prague, but that was childish. I decided to give a concert to show him that not only I was a god with a fiddle, but the patron violinist of Bohemia. He would know that I am my father's son, come hell or high water. And when he saw me at my peak, he would leave the orchestra and never look back. I spoke to a friend of mine, a pianist and impresario who went by the stage name, Count Fugue. We arranged to do a gala concert, but we just needed a theater. Fugue would work on that, I just needed to focus on playing. Finding the right piece to play wasn't much of a challenge, since we scrapped the idea of doing the Dvorak Concerto again. I decided to do something more challenging, something to set me apart from the rest, and

I knew just the thing; I would perform all of Paganini's Caprices in one show.

The night afterward, I dug up a volume of the sheet music and began to practice. For days leading up to the gala, I lived, slept and smoked Paganini. I woke up at the crack of dawn, did push-ups and showered, and practiced for an hour and a half. I ate, then went straight back to practicing for another two hours. I took a break for a while then practiced for another six hours. I ended each day with dinner and a trip to meet and have sex with Janina to get the lead out. As I toiled like a Hebrew slave at this task, Count Fugue set to work getting the word out to the public. No matter how many times I asked where the show would take place, he would always tell me he hadn't found a theatre.

On the day leading up to the big event, I practiced little and just spent the day with my muse drinking and fucking. I was feeling like Caesar before storming off to battle Ptolemy, standing by the window drinking wine straight from the bottle while my Cleopatra teased me.

"You're so full of yourself, maestro!" Janina said lazily, slithering out of the bedsheets.

"I ought to be, I'm God's fiddler, after-all!" I said, taking a long swig from the wine bottle. "Soon, the city will know that, and after this city, the world!"

Janina laughed. "Of course, of course! Nobody plays Paganini like you, love! But be warned, power like that will go to your head before you know it." With that, we finished the last of the wine and went back to bed like a couple of rabbits. When we were done, Janina sang a high-C as we melted into the sweaty mattress.

Later that morning, around 10:30, we sat down to a fry-up and coffee. Just as we finished, Count Fugue came knocking at my door, finally he had the right venue that would take me, and I didn't even have to audition for it. The show was going to be held at the National Theatre this very evening at seven. With that, I was forced into the shower and squeezed into my bowtie and tailcoat. Janina even combed my hair for me like I was some kind of toddler violin prodigy. While she stayed home to do her own primping and pampering for the gala, my friend and I took a cab to the theater, where a red carpet was laid out in front, supposedly a brass band was going to play as people came in. I was then escorted into the backstage area by my friend and the manager; the theatre staff were hard at work; the stage was being mopped and the auditorium was being swept.

I didn't do any last-minute practicing that night. I was actually so sick of Paganini I was beating myself up for taking on the challenge. Yet by now, I knew the 24 Caprices in my muscles. It was torture doing just a few of these over and over, especially the final caprice everyone knew. These people were in for a show, but all of the sudden I began to panic; what if I displaced one note while playing? Hell, what if a string broke or I drew blood on the E-string? Here's the son of a renowned conductor-pianist, and the protégé of Lipchitz and steward of a Stradivarius, making a jackass of himself onstage in front of royalty.

I would bring shame to Dvorak and now Paganini, let alone the City of Prague, the Vienna of the East, all of this made me insane. Under all of this I sat on the sofa in this dressing room for an hour, until out of nowhere there was a knock on the door. "20 minutes till curtain, maestro!"

I wasn't terribly hungry, but to prevent myself from going completely insane, I scarfed down a banana, which I would always do before going onstage. I always played better on a full stomach. I stepped outside of the dressing room and took a peek through the curtain. It was a full house, and the brass band was still playing outside. My friend came out and told me to wait offstage, he was dressed in his finest tailcoat and a red brocaded vest with a tie to match. He looked like a magician. With that, at rise the brass band was now in the auditorium, and joined by a drummer. They played the Toccata from Orfeo, which silenced the audience immediately. That being done, my friend took center stage and gave an elaborate speech, I wasn't paying attention at all, I just stood there, instrument in hand waiting to shine. Out of nowhere, the audience gave a round of applause and began singing the national anthem.

I was then ushered onstage, under a bright spotlight that obstructed my view of the audience. Their applause was deafening. I've never experienced stage-fright until this one show. I gave only a slight bow, lifted my Strad under my chin, and started playing nonstop. I played each frenzied Caprice, one by one with only a few seconds in between the next. As I got to the 20th, all I could hear was a humming in the silence, and soon I could only hear my heart and lungs as if I were having a palpitation. I was sweating profusely, and my neat pompadour was flying across my face in damp locks. There where bow-hair's flying all over the place, and I stopped only to pluck them off once. My mouth was going dry, and I was swaying and dancing a little on the spot. Finally as I started the infamous 24th Caprice, I could feel the audience's anticipation, this was the shit or miss moment. I could feel this piece in the muscles of my left hand. Once I was finally done, I heard a rush of maddening applause. The house lights went on and people where giving me a standing ovation. The sudden change in the light made me see stars, I was starting to lose my composure. I collapsed right there on the spot, luckily I didn't drop my violin. Somehow, a stagehand managed to catch it before it fell on the stage and broke.

When I woke up, I was sprawled on a couch in my dressing room where a doctor was looming over me. The performance was a success. As I boasted, the city recognized me as the virtuoso I was, and I was enjoying my fifteen minutes of fame. But the power went to my head, and my ego got the most of me. To my selfish mind, I was the alpha and the omega, no other musician was my equal. Things got slightly better, and I was happy again, for a little while. For Janina and me, happiness no longer revolved in the arts, but in material gain. I was always spending money on the finest suits, but I spent most of my money on the one thing that really got me and other musicians going, cocaine. At the time, cocaine was the thing of kings, and soon enough, I and Janina were hooked.

I always kept a little stash of the goods in a cigarette case, where I packed a bag and snuffer, and a razor blade if I needed to cut it up. Everywhere I went, things revolved around two things only; the violin and cocaine. It got to a point where my daily bread consisted of coffee, cognac, sex and cocaine. I'd get up in the morning, exercise, do a line, shower, shave, do a snuff, eat, have sex with Janina, then we'd both do a line, practice, lunch, practice again, performance, do another line, drink cognac, and then sleep. Sometimes when the rush of cocaine kept me up, I'd take these sleeping pills Janina's doctor prescribed and I'd be out like a light.

As for Janina, things between us slowly began to go sour. Our bohemian romance was a thing of the past now that we were living like royalty. Janina's character was what deteriorated the most, and living in the status quo of high society gave her the power high she craved. However, this power is what made her cool, collected character heat up in a swirling maelstrom of selfishness, greed and anxiety. The cocaine and her doctor's prescribed anxiety medication didn't help, in fact, that's what made it worse.

Janina went from a free-spirited bohemian to a prima donna. She would always go on a shopping binge, buying the latest dresses, shoes and overpriced goodies money can buy. I wasn't very rich, but with my inheritance from my father and my high income from playing the violin, we had a pot to piss in and a window to throw it out of; granted, the pot was ivory and the window was the top floor penthouse in New Town, Prague. At some point, we had it in mind to move to Chicago or New York, but this never happened. Looking back, I'm glad it didn't, and here's why.

Janina's transformation from free spirit to rich man's wife, as well as her own addictions, bought out the worst of her personal demons. In fact, she was showing her true character; day by day she became spoiled, self-indulgent, and more of a trophy than a lover. Much to my surprise, whenever I made any money, she would always get her greedy hands on it first. Whenever we traveled or attended concerts, dinner or any reception, she always came dolled up in her latest outfit, painting herself as this perfect goddess while she rotted from the inside. She was no longer my muse but a demanding, verbally abusive bitch. Whenever she didn't have any money to blow away, it was my fault. If she couldn't have a line coke, it was my fault. If I couldn't stay home because it was her cat's birthday, it was my fault. If I got up to get my morning papers and she was in a bad mood because of it, that was my fault. If I was too tired to fuck her, it was my fault. And the list goes on, and always kept getting longer.

The worst of Janina's ticks where her constant accusations of me cheating on her, even though I hadn't been out getting laid since we first got together. I swear on my mother's grave, I had been keeping it in my pants, never touching another woman except by the hand. The only pussy I would get was from Janina, anyway, and now she was forcing me to grovel at her feet like a dog, all for sins I never committed. Besides, I had to be away to keep a roof over her head, and money in her greedy hands. But to Janina, my work didn't matter, I was a lazy prick who never worked a day in his life, a drug-fiend and a sex hound. She didn't see the virtuoso, but a magic piggy-bank that would never run dry.

Whenever Janina was in a rage, berating and abusing me for the most absurd reason, I numbed myself with more cocaine and cognac, no longer caring that the muse I once worshiped was bringing about my own damnation. I was too proud to care and too numb on the inside to take any action. What did I care, anyway? I was living on easy street, I had more money than I could ask for in a lifetime and a trophy wife, even though we never married. Thank God.

But eventually, when the high wore off, that's when the shit hit the fan. While I was working day and night, practicing, performing and rubbing shoulders with the musical big-wigs of Europe, Janina was living a double-life. When I wasn't enough to satisfy her lustful needs, other men where there, and she was like a kid in a candy store. Any sleaze in a bar who could buy her a drink would be the first to get up her skirt, and as long as I wasn't home, Janina would bring her lovers to the same bed where I slept. By dawn, the sheets would be washed and Janina would wash away her sins in the shower as if nothing happened.

Everything came crashing down like the Philistine Palace, and I blame myself for turning the other cheek. After fucking like a maniac, Janina got pregnant, and supposedly I was the father. At first, I was terrified of the concept of bringing a child into the world, but I manned up and felt proud to have a son of my own, somebody to pass on my legacy. I was looking at myself in the mirror, seeing a spitting-image of my father, how alike he and I were and soon I could have the kind of musical family I grew up with. But had my father been alive to see the full picture, he would have died all over again from shock.

His grandson (or daughter) was not his descendant but a fraud. At first, I didn't think this baby was a bastard, but my ego kept me from investigating. I was doing everything in my power to make sure my kid was welcome at home, but everything stopped with a bang. According to Janina, she miscarried. She was only three months pregnant and she lost the baby. I was devastated, too numb to mourn, and in my selfish heart I now saw everything fall into place. I knew in the back of my mind that my muse was a filthy, greedy whore, but I shut it all away.

Eventually, as she wept in my arms over the loss of the brat in her womb, she never shed any actual tears. In fact, Janina was only pitying herself above all others, and soon we started fighting. Right then and there, Janina spilled out the truth. It wasn't my child, it was some random sleaze she met at a bar's child. And that wasn't a miscarriage, it was an abortion. Janina murdered the unborn child to cover everything up, and now she wanted another from me as if nothing happened. I never laid a hand on a woman before, but in a fit of rage I hit her. I gave that devil in a black dress a hard, back-handed slap that knocked her over and everything went to hell.

Janina lunged right back up and started bighting and clawing like a madwoman, and the chaos alerted our neighbors below. The police came and I spent the night in remand, and after hours of talking to the police and a lawyer, things settled themselves out. Unfortunately, no trial was held since Janina and I never married, so we settled things as follows. I got the hell away from that cheating bitch as quickly as I could. I packed up a suitcase, grabbed my violin, took as much money as I could get away from her before she robbed me dry, and left. I had enough money to get by for a few years, and as long as I closed my bank account and re-opened a new one, Janina would have to kill me to get my money.

I let her keep the penthouse, though. But she sold it and went back to the bars, living among the same gypsies and other lowlifes she knew before she was rich. Whether or not she ever sang again is up for debate, but as long as she was out of my life, we were both satisfied. She was content to live a decedent lifestyle, with or without me and as long as her filthy, black heart kept beating.

For some time, I was glad to be rid of Janina, but soon the heartache and grief she inflicted boiled up and killed me from the inside. Soon enough, I stopped performing altogether, music meant nothing to me anymore. For weeks, all I really cared about was getting my next fix to ease the pain. However, drugs and alcohol weren't enough. While hanging around the chaps at the bar, I got sucked into the world of gambling, especially poker. I would frequent the poker table on a weekly basis, sometimes coming out with a thousand crowns or more, and overtime, I was making more money than I made as a musician. The power of capital was a high cocaine couldn't match, and I was living the high life again.

Soon enough, I went down a hole of my own making, of gambling, whores, cocaine and soon I was not the one consuming, but I was introduced to a new trade, the trade of drug peddling. Long story short, one of the jobs I was involved with went wrong, and soon me and my cohorts were arrested and imprisoned. I was let off after a few months. But, to my dumb luck and hot-headed nature, I was back in jail again. This time, I got into a drunken brawl with some scumbag who tried to cheat me out of a deal, and the chaos escalated into a war of fists and broken glass. When the smoke cleared, I was hauled into the drunk tank, fined and let off with another slap on the wrist, but the police kept an eye on me from then on.

As I hid in my new apartment in the city, I slowly felt the high of it all wear off. I became what I grew to hate; I was no longer an artist, I was now a complete lowlife. A bum, a drunk, a total libertine. But at least I wasn't poor, yet that didn't matter. They say money can't buy happiness, now I knew what that meant. The world would never see me as the virtuoso who played half as good as Paganini, Vivaldi, Kreisler or any other composer. The fact that I had a Stradivarius made no difference, either. The steward of this prized instrument was a loser, first class. This is what I saw in the mirror whenever I shaved in the morning. Sometimes, I wondered if I used the razor to end my life, things would be better, the world would be fine without a failure like me. This though manifested one morning when I got out of the shower, grabbed the razor and slit my wrist. Fortunately, I didn't die. The door was unlocked and the landlord found me bleeding on the cold, tile floor. After a week in the hospital, I decided to just accept life as it was, and just let nature kill me first. Suicide wasn't worth it, so I packed my bags once more and got on the metro. I rode for half an hour until I reached the end of the line, far away from the city of Prague and the one-horse town where I live now. I won't tell you the real name of this neighborhood, I'll just call it what it is, the rightful name of the dark hole I dug myself into; Skid Row.

Well, there you have it! That's the jest of how I got to where I am now, from high society to the underground, from heaven to hell. Now that you know my sob story, let's get back to the real one, I'm sure you don't want to be bored any further.

III

The second I left the flat, the cold hit me. Boris's death must have really bought this neighborhood down. The last happy man in the world was dead. I only had one thing on my mind, the same thing when my father died; a damn cigarette. Just like then, I was out of smokes.

I was listening for a boyish-alto voice singing Korobushka, hopefully the girl singing it had some Pall-Malls or Dunghills in her trey. In the stillness, I couldn't hear it. I started down the street from my building, going in the direction of the whorehouses. If anybody needed cigarettes at this hour, it's the poor broads grinding away with the sleaziest of the sleazes for a living. Not only was she not there, but all the crimson-lit windows where empty. Boris's death must have affected the ladies of the night, as well. However, standing in the Corinthian-pillared doorway of the hotel was Natasha the Courtesan, smoking her fancy cigarillo out of a long holder.

She was dressed in a rabbit-fur coat over her bodice and stockings, and despite the chill she wore it open to advertise the goods. She prided herself as the best escort in town, and the faint wrinkles on her face suggested she knew the business of prostitution well enough, but in reality it showed just how used up she was despite the layer of makeup. She had dirty blonde hair halfway down to her heart-shaped ass, and covered the bagginess in her eyes with violet eyeshadow, and kept her .38 revolver in a holster within reach. Natasha had enemies in this town, and didn't play around when her life and business was under siege by many an envious pimp.

"Mind if I bum a cigarette?" I asked her.

"F'eh, you musicians are all the same!" She said, blowing a smoke-ring at me. "If you'd play me a song for once I'll let you have the whole pack! Where's you fiddle?"

"I sold it for booze money."

"And you couldn't get some of your own cigarettes?"

"Smoked them all for dinner last night."

"Well poor you, Maestro! I tell you, when I was courted by the late Eduard Strauss, he at least smoked his own after a round with me!"

"Oh really? Did he take you out to the ball first or was it straight to bed with him?"

"Oh yes, we waltzed, we dined with royalty, we drank champagne, we fucked, we had the whole Vienna experience! And he played a special waltz for me at the ball."

"One just for you! One of the Strauss's wrote a waltz for you? How did it go?" I asked sarcastically, there was no way in hell a Strauss brother would date someone as lowly as Natasha. But I could be wrong. Natasha laughed and hummed a tune in her tobacco-altered voice, but something sounded fishy.

"Hold on, that's Chit-Chat by Johann Strauss, and that's not even a waltz it's a polka!"

"Well don't you know your music, Maestro?" Natasha said, blowing a smoke ring. "Why don't you come inside for a while and maybe we'll talk more about it. Nobody wanders down this block alone without looking for a date, you know."

"Maybe that's why I'm here, and maybe some cigarettes while I'm at it." With that, she beckoned me into the hotel, leading me through the dimly lit foyer and up the stairs where her suite was. On the brocaded walls there where framed pictures, everything from photos of the women moaning away behind the closed doors to plates from Marquis de Sade books. Behind one door guarded by the Madame running the hotel, I heard a man's muffled cries as a boorish lady flogged him.

Finally, Natasha led me to her private room; in the center there was a bed with a thick purple duvet, along which were scattered a bunch of throw-pillows. The room, despite the open French window, was alive with the smell of incense and spunk from other customers. "Have a seat on the bed, Maestro, let me change into something more comfortable."

With that, I took off my jacket and flung it lazily over a coat hanger next to her wardrobe which was shut with a padlock. I looked around the space lit by gaslights which gave the place a faint orange tint, complementing the brocaded wallpaper that reflected the light. There was a print of Caravaggio's 'Sick Bacchus' on one wall and on the opposite, there was an icon of Michelangelo's 'Pieta' which had two unlit candles hanging on each side. There was a rack full of whips, floggers, paddles and a bunch of other lotions and potions in phials. I kicked my shoes off and sat down on the bed, and within a minute, Natasha re-entered; she was now wearing a bodice and fishnets, and around all this she wore a large, furry boa that dragged across the floor.

With a catlike strut, Natasha sat on my lap and immediately began to work as if her next meal depended on it. Flinging the boa around me and undoing my tie, she began to kiss my neck, and as I returned the favor, the animal libido within me went off like an engine on full power. For the next half hour, we fucked. It was as if nothing else mattered that I felt a realization that something in my life was missing, but ten minutes into the escapade, the passion faded into simple, trudging mechanics. Sex with Natasha was as lame as with any prostitute in Skid Row.

When half an hour was up, I laid back on the purple duvet feeling as if I would fall asleep. The gratification was brief, but vanished once I realized Natasha was lying next to me, mounting me from above and kissing me on the lips. Now getting a better look at her, she was a lot older than she looked outside the hotel. "That will be fifteen Koruna, Maestro." She said lazily.

Reaching for my wallet, I paid her without counting twice, a habit I've grown a custom to when paying whores. Natasha sat there languidly, still naked counting her tribute and hastily stuffed it in her left stocking. As if I wasn't there, she silently dismissed me and I left the hotel still buttoning my shirt and redoing my tie. Throughout my life with all my escapades with the fair sex, I've come to this conclusion; there are three kinds of sex- good, bad and mediocre. Often times, good sex is a rarity among the bad sex. The only women in my life who lived up to my standards of good sex was the cocktail waitress that took my virginity at nineteen and the devil herself, Janina. Bad sex is merely coitus no better than masturbating in bed or in the shower, whereas mediocre sex is like bad sex but just lazier, sloppier and completely devoid of lust, just the compulsive drive for an orgasm no matter how mediocre the experience. What happened with Natasha was just a step above mediocre, but did little to make me feel any happier.

As I stood on the cold porch of the hotel, I reached in my pocket for my pack of smokes and found it empty. I resumed my search for cigarettes, turning the corner of the red-light district and into the street that the locals around Skid Row call 'Hell Hole.' This is a fitting name for such a street; it's one of the dingiest, darkest, rat infested streets where everything goes to die. From the bums who drink themselves to death to the johns who die from clap to the premature children of the whores in the red-light district.

When I was a kid, my father used to scare the living shit out of me with tales of the Black Plague, and Hell Hole to me was the living embodiment of his stories. However, tonight I was too numbed of all feeling to run for cover. I just didn't care if a flea bit me in the ass and infected me with the plague. I could see it now; pus-filled lesions and lumps on my body, coughing up bloody phlegm, constant diarrhea and vomiting, and all the fun stuff. My landlady would probably evict me so I don't spread my disease to the rest of the building and cast me to die in the gutters of Hell Hole. Indiscriminately, I took a casual stroll down the block, seeing that a light was on in one of the buildings and Dolf the Pimp was leaning against the lamppost.

"Funny I should see you here, Maestro!" He said lighting a cigarette. It was unlike Dolf to greet me so cordially. Normally the man would loom over me like impending doom whenever he saw me, especially with one of his whores whom he treated like slaves. Hell, he'd do the same if I was around any women in public as if he were the sharia police. Dolf was anything but a gentleman and a scholar. He was mean, vulgar, and hardly showered or shaved. To him a splash of Joup Cologne counted as a bath, he worked too hard to bathe properly. He kept his unkempt red hair in a ponytail and his fat belly tucked under a dirty vest. He had big, muscular arms like Bluto, Popeye's nemesis, and kept his mousy goatee waxed in a long, straight fashion. The man also prided himself on having the best whores and the best drugs in town, if not the best in all of Czechoslovakia. For such fine women, these were some of the most miserable, robotic women I ever knew. A lot of these women would be seen out in public beaten and bruised, not bothering to cover their wounds with makeup, which would diminish their market-value and get them more beatings. Dolf would clobber them with the wooden truncheon he kept in his belt, it was his symbol of authority, the fist of God. Any whore that didn't pull their weight would get a proper beating with that fucking thing, and sometimes he'd miss and hit them where it could be seen. It was not uncommon for a john who tried to rip him off to get a few bones broken, either.

Once any lady got a taste of his hashish or pills, Dolf owned them for life, and often had to go back to him to work for their next fix. For some odd reason the man was obsessed with me, being a well-known musician, therefore I had money and he wanted it. He just didn't have the balls to steal it knowing I had once fired my pistol at one of his goons who snuck into my apartment.

"Good evening, Dolf, I see you are working hard tonight." I said coolly.

"All in a good night's work, I've got a customer who paid for a four-hour session with little Magda."

Hearing that name, I wanted to go in there and save the poor girl. But it was too late. Little Magda was one of the younger whores in training, and half the size of a normal nineteen-year-old woman. But just like all of Dolf's harem, she was his property for life, and whatever beauty she had was being sucked out of her by some scumbag living in the ruins of Hell Hole, Skid Row.

"Four hours," I said. "Whoever's up there must have paid you good money for that."

Dolf grinned, showing his yellow teeth. With that he flashed a stack of cash. "150 gulden, that's what I call a good night's work, little Magda's getting fed well tonight. If you're looking for a lay, Maestro, I'd come back tomorrow, I'm afraid the poor girl's gonna be tired after such a long session and all the others are getting the club for not pulling their weight."

"I have a dose of clap, my good man, I don't think I'll be fucking anytime soon, I'm afraid."

Dolf laughed a snorting pig-like guffaw. "Mighty sorry to hear that, Maestro! A strapping young lad such as yourself ought to be clean and fucking like crazy, but I guess it'll happen to anybody. Ye' know, I might just have the thing that'll ease your pain, perhaps some hashish will do you good?"

"No, I'm afraid I can't stand the stuff, makes me sluggish. Perhaps you have something stronger?" this was probably the stupidest thing I ever asked. Now the man would own me for life, but I was too stupid to care.

Dolf scratched his beard as he thought. "Hmm, I do, but nobody's bought it from me before. I've never tried the stuff myself, to be honest but it will get you really high on just one dose!" With that, he reached into his vest pocket and took out a glass phial the size of a large pill.

"Just put a drop of this on a cigarette or a sugar cube, and you're all set."

"Very well," I said. "How much for a drop?"

"Two gulden, I'll throw in a cigarette for free!"

"Sold."

With that, Dolf took a cigarette out of his pack and dipped it in the phial. I paid the man and went to the park to smoke up. Satisfied that I finally had a damn cigarette, I lit up and sat back on a park bench under a gaslight. The tobacco tasted like turpentine. After a few more puffs, things started to get weird, and fast. The gold color of the gaslight started to warm me up but the color started to flood the damask blue park, and soon all the dull colors became oversaturated. Once I finished the drugged stogie, I sat rooted to the spot, hallucinating. All that surrounded me became augmented into a surreal reality that amazed and terrified me at the same time. The crickets singing became an eerie white-noise that bombarded my ears to a point where the little chirps sounded like double-basses. Colors and patterns where swimming and the ground started to bubble like a vat of syrup. The gas light stretched and bent over, then it went out. I sat in the darkness, my head spinning and my body began to levitate. I looked up into the pitch-black sky. It was cloudy that night, so the sky looked like a void, and in that void, I now knew what Nietzsche meant about staring into an abyss. In the blackness of the sky, I saw rippling spirals dance in the ether, and in the center of these eight black tendrils appeared. In the center of the wiggling tendrils, I saw a huge red eye that gazed into my very soul. This was it, now I really was damned for all eternity, I thought. With that, I closed my eyes and passed out on the spot.

At this point in my trip, the darkness went white. I wasn't curled up on a wooden bench in a cold park but in a white linen bed, naked as the day I was born. I was sweating slightly and I opened my eyes. I was completely silent as a sexy, dark-haired goddess loomed over me. She looked at me with her green-hazel eyes and grabbed my chin in a vice-grip. Only one woman I knew would do that, and now she suddenly came back to taunt me.

"You haven't lived until you love a goddess." She whispered. And with that, she stood over me and lifted her slender, dirty foot over my face, and started to crush me with it. For some time she stomped on me and I could almost feel the bones in my chest crack, but I felt no real pain. This continued for some time until the drugs wore off.

I awoke curled up on the bench. I checked my watch to find I had only been out for 35 minutes. That was the longest half hour in my life. I was cold and my fingers where turning blue, so I got off my cold ass to seek shelter. That funky cigarette did nothing to make me any happier, even if it made me see an octopus in the sky. In the stillness, I wandered with my head down until I ended up in another end of town nobody ever visits, the church.

It was a typical gothic-style cathedral, dimly lit by candles. Nobody was there tonight, not even the priest. People rarely went there even for Sunday mass, so the priest would often say mass to an empty church. I sat down in the front pew by the altar, which was just a few candles and a large icon of the Black Madonna. The organ started to play itself. It played Bach's 'Hertzlich thut mich Verlangen,' but in a very melancholic tone that seemed different than how it was intended to sound by the composer. Rather than a call to God, it seemed more like a person riddled with heartache that couldn't be satisfied, as if no mortal woman could heal such pain. Perhaps the organ was looking for a proper organist to play it but the musicians in town were no match. The organ was pleading to Bach's spirit in its dissatisfaction with the old lady who usually played it.

Out of the blackness, a young woman in a traditional Czech costume emerged. She was ghostly white and had red eyes like rubies. Now I knew I was dead or dying, this was The Goddess Persephone, the wife of Pluto who came to seduce me, to taunt me in my damnation. But she looked at me with a happy gleam in her pale face that made her glow like a beacon. She stood in the center of the altar, and began to sing. I've heard some great sopranos in my time, but this was divine. She was singing the national anthem, accompanied by the organ, and loud enough to fill a stadium.

With one drawn out 'D' at the end of her song, the red-eyed vixen vanished. I sat there mouth-agape, wishing she would come back. I wanted to call out to her but I was tongue-tied. Something was waking me up like I'd been resurrected from death. I checked my pulse and found it still beating, I wasn't seeing colors or stars either, so the drugged cigarette defiantly wore off. Now I needed a cold beer more than anything, and hearing the national anthem stirred up some kind of national pride, and it's well known that we Czechs love a good beer to a point that we drink more on average than any other nation, even Germany.

I left the church and headed back to town square, where Pesak's pub was. From outside, I could hear the gutter-roll of a battered accordion playing a polka and the stomping of feet on the wood, nutshell ridden floor. It sounded more like a funeral dirge than a polka. When I went in, the bar was filled with the smoke of many cigars, cigarettes and pipes, and it smelled of fresh prasky and fried cheese patties. In the center, people where skipping about lazily to the beat of the accordion, and a sausage maker was selling his wear in a corner by the counter. I ordered a pint and found a place to sit. Vaklav was sitting in the rear booth as usual, all by himself and nursing a neat scotch. I took a seat by him and we had a light chat, there was a lot on my mind but having a good chat with Vaklav was abnormal. He was too drunk to say much anyway, and was always known around town as a remorseful drunkard.

Something was different about him, though, Vaklav had a black eye and there was tape around the bridge of his glasses. "So, got yourself into another political debate?" I asked. He replied with only a grunt and took a swig of his whiskey.

"You ask too many questions, sometimes. You know that?" He said.

"Well, I'm within my right to ask, nobody says you have to answer!"

"That's the problem with you, Franz! You're under the influence of the Americans and their imperialist propaganda. All of those times you lived among Americans, they poisoned your brain with their decedent lifestyle of consumerism and the Protestant Work Ethic."

"What the hell are you talking about?" I said putting my beer down.

"I'm talking about the truth, Franz!" He said, wagging his index finger. "It is written in Das Kapital and the Manifesto that 'Property is Theft! The American and the European alike are slaves to their capital, so much that we care little for the wellbeing of others, all to a point where we steal from the needy with our commerce. That, my friend is why you are as corrupt as the Americans."

From here I decided to just keep my mouth shut, before things got out of hand. Vaklav was already sitting there, lips puckered and arms folded smugly as if he had won a debate. I decided to just let him have his fun. I only wanted to ask him a simple question and here he is lecturing me about Marxist Economics. Of course, part of me wanted to remind him that the Americans gave us the foundation for our own national sovereignty as Czechs, but he would only argue further.

Out of nowhere, the music stopped and people sat in silence drinking. As I sat there, the stench of body-odor and Joup cologne filled my nostrils as a hairy hand clad in rings grabbed my shoulder. "So, it seems the fiddler has returned!" A raspy voice said. I looked around and saw that Moshe was looming over me as his watchdog Dolf sat down next to us.

"Pleasure seeing you, Moshe." I said taking a drink of beer.

"The same to you, Maestro!" Said Moshe. "I understand you tried some of Dolf's elixir, how did it work for you?"

"I found God." I said.

"Really, now? What does he look like?"

"I couldn't tell you, no man can describe him."

At this statement, Vaklav tried to butt in. "Maestro!"

"Quiet you!" Moshe said.

"Yeah, the man says he found God, let him speak!" Said Dolf. "You ought to try it yourself, Commie!"

"Ay! Leave him alone you god-damned brute!" I shouted. With this, the two mobsters turned on me, we all stood up ready to fight, tooth and claw. The three of us where armed, I had my father's .22 revolver in a holster under my jacket, Moshe always packed a .45 magnum in his belt while Dolf was the only one who didn't carry a firearm regularly, just that wooden head- knocker he used on his whores. Normally he kept a loaded shotgun in his harem, but that was something he used on the Johns who tried to cheat him.

"Divine madness." Moshe said with a leer. "It can be a dangerous thing when put in the wrong hands. It seems God has put it in the hands of a playboy like you, Franz!"

"I'm not a playboy, I'm an artist!" I said, my temper rising.

"Sure, you are." Moshe said sarcastically. "Next thing you want to tell me you're a priest."

"You watch yourself, kike!" I grunted. With that, the entire room went silent, the tension was thick. Nobody in the pub dared to breathe or cough. Nobody in Skid Row had ever stood up to a bully like Moshe or any of his gang. Dolf, however, made to attack me but Moshe elbowed him back.

"Don't mind him, Dolf," Moshe said still keeping his glassy eyes on me. "I'll let that little insult slide, but one more and I'll give the fiddler hell to pay. We already wasted our energy on the cigarette girl, anyway."

"What did you say?" I said.

"Maestro, shush!" Vaklav blurted.

"Nothing much." Dolf said. "We only collected some of her debts."

With that, he opened his vest under which he had stuffed several packs of cigarettes and lighters. I looked over at the booth where a group of thugs were sitting and they were passing around a wooden trey of loot. I recognized this as the trey of goods the Cigarette Girl carried around, and it dawned on me that the thieves were passing around a moth-eaten scarf and a worn-out pair of boots.

"What have you done to her?" I demanded.

"Relax, maestro!" Said Moshe in a false calming voice. "Like we said, we only collected a debt she owed, she's fine!"

With that I strode out of the bar and went looking for the Cigarette Girl, frantically searching every alley and gangway. It wasn't long until I went back to the same park bench where I took Dolf's drugged cigarette only to hear the sound of somebody whimpering in the darkness.

The Cigarette Girl was there alright, sprawled on the ground as if dead. She was beaten and bruised and all of her cigarettes where gone, her money was also stolen from her pockets. Her face was bruised and cut in a few places, her dirty blonde hair was a mess under her little newsboy cap. The bastards who left her like this even stole her jacket and shoes, leaving her long sweaty feet to turn blue in the cold. She had no socks to begin with, save some tattered cloth wrapped around her feet. Yet they didn't bother to take her hat and fingerless gloves.

She was only seventeen yet had to grow up on the streets of this miserable town with nobody. Humbled, I picked her up and took her back to my apartment. Ms. Krovar was there and without question helped me, seeing the poor girl in such a dire state. I put her down on the sofa as the landlady got a hot washcloth and bandages. She also got a pair of stockings and immediately covered the Cigarette Girl's cold, bare feet and started treating her wounds.

IV

I watched over the Cigarette Girl as she lay in my bed. I barely slept a wink myself, since I had been consoling her most of the night. Ms. Krovar let her bathe and washed her cloths, and gave her a new pair of shoes from her own rack. Although she desperately wanted to go back to her garret, the Landlady insisted on nursing her. It turns out, she lived in an attic garret where she only had a mattress and crates full of cigars, cigarettes and snuff and a vault of cash. She managed to prevent Dolf from stealing her keys, thankfully.

At some point I took a nap on my own sofa and slept till noon. While I slept, the Cigarette Girl was having tea with the Landlady and was invited to stay with her. I woke up and went to my room to get a proper sleep, but something prevented me from taking off my cloths and getting under the covers. I looked under my bed and for the first time in a year and a half, I dragged out a long, leather case. There were two other parcels next to it, a case with a revolver and ammo and a safe where I kept all my money. This particular case was the most valuable of them all.

I placed the case on the bed and opened it. My violin was still in there, and surprisingly still in tune. I picked up the instrument, hooked on the shoulder rest, and began to play. I played Sibelius' Violin Concerto, my favorite piece. As I played, I turned to see Ms. Krovar and the Cigarette Girl in my doorway, both of whom had tears in their eyes.

I was feeling a spark I hadn't felt in years, not since my 15 minutes of fame after the Paganini concert. I began to play some more and went into the landlady's parlor where I continued to play. The couple next door, hearing the music, stopped their fighting and came in to hear me play. Soon enough, more people came in to hear it. Word got out and soon enough we had to move outside to the yard. The Cigarette Girl and I decided to make a profit out of this, so we threw a little ball in the yard.

First, we cleaned some of the garbage and rubble out of the yard while the women busied themselves with decorating the area with garden lanterns. A makeshift dancefloor was placed near the stack of creates that would serve as the bandstand. We had a band which included myself, the Cigarette Girl and two other singers, an accordion, a bass, a trombone, a clarinet and a guitarist. People bought food and three kegs of beer and wine, and the sausage maker even came to sell his ware. After a while, the Cigarette Girl stopped to join the dancers, where she waltzed with the Shoe-shining Boy, whom she loved. For the first time in what seemed like ages, people in Skid Row where happy. I was actually happy.

After a while, the musicians took a break to eat and drink. To keep the music going, Ms. Krovar played a few records, and people continued to dance on the slabs of plywood near the stage. One by one, more kegs of beer came in from the Old Brewery, and the ball continued well into the night. By one in the morning, people where good and drunk, their bellies where full and there was music in Skid Row for what seemed like the first time in a century.

The musicians and I were paid well, our pockets filled with tips, and soon we would be doing this more often. In the heat of the moment, I took to the stage and decided to give the evening a good finale. People went silent as I began to play Bach's Chaconne. Everyone stared in awe as if they had never heard such a beautiful tune before, and I could see that some people where in tears as the Chaconne slowed to a melancholic mood, then sat on the edge of their seats as I played the faster, ill-tempered arpeggios non-stop. Then the tension of the crowd became relaxed as the Chaconne took a serene tone, slow then gradually faster.

Then just as I was about to finish with a few more brisk chords, all hell broke loose in the yard. There was a defining bang from a man wielding a pistol who rushed into the yard, along with five other thugs who started tearing the place apart. People either ducked for cover or tried vainly to defend themselves as more thugs came pouring in, all of whom were wearing masks or bandanas and brandishing weapons. Only two of the men had fire-arms and the rest had wither clubs, pipes or some kind of blunt object at their disposal.

The man with a pistol fired three more shots into the air, madly cackling as more people screamed and ran for cover. Leaping into the fray, I tackled the gunman and started to beat him to a pulp. With one pull on his wrist, I managed to wrench a pistol out of his hand, then I knocked him out with a swift pistol/whip. My hands were covered with blood and I began to feel a hot surge or rage fill me as I grabbed the other pistol and pocketed it, now hell bent on fighting back.

The other masked thugs were too busy to help their fallen comrade, as the yard became a bloody pandemonium of brawls and broken bones, it was every man for himself. Out of the corner of my eye, I saw one masked man chasing a group of screaming women with a loaded shotgun, and that's what set me off like a madman. I ran up to the man and shot him directly in the ass, and he went down like a sack of bricks, almost completely silent from the shock. If he was lucky to survive, he'd be crippled for life.

I tried my damnedest to help usher the women to safety, but one wouldn't move from the spot where she stood, screaming her lungs horse as the others tried to get her to move. After a lot of coaxing, I took off my jacket so she could shield herself and I helped them get her out of the yard. Just when I thought things couldn't escalate any further, there was a defending blast that shook the yard to the core. There was a blood curdling scream as the masked thugs fled the scene of the crime, somebody was either mortally wounded or dead, and what we all saw in the back of the yard confirmed the source of the scream.

The shoeshine boy was murdered in cold blood. His brains where splattered against the wall and there was a chunk of wood still clutched limply in his hand, as if he died in battle. The Cigarette Girl was curled in a corner crying, she had been the one who screamed and now over people where either still cowering or trying to get her out of the yard as the police came.

I just stood there frozen. I had seen death plenty of times in my life but nothing like this, nothing as innocent as a child this young. The hot rage of the battle reared up in me as I started running out toward the street, desperate to do onto the bastard who pulled the trigger.

The murderers where gone, back to the slimy holes they slithered out of. "Murderers!" I screamed. "Murderers! Mother fucking murderers!" my scream reverberated like a war cry in the silence, and none of the cowards would show their faces. The abyss that was Skid Row was staring back, mocking me like a childish demon wielding a plastic sword. This was the final straw. As God and Czechoslovakia my whiteness, I would not let those god damned monsters get away with this. I knew who these men where, none other than Moshe, Dolf and their cronies who ran this neighborhood like dictators, and nobody in this neighborhood, especially the police, where willing to risk their lives to stop them.

If anybody was to do anything to teach these murderers the law of lex talionis, I was going to do that. I just needed to round up a posse. It would be suicide to face these murderers alone, and I knew just the right men to join me. Men who had seen battle on the frontlines, men who had lost faith in the law and where out for revenge. Before long, I had spoken with the bartender who served in the army and it didn't take much to convince him to join me, he had been at odds with Moshe for years and this raid of the ball was the last nail in the coffin for him. Luckily he was armed, he always kept his rifle strapped underneath the bar, as he was prone to robbery.

Another man who would be joining me was the trombonist, who was always passed out at the bar and served in the army, but was discharged for gross negligence of duty. He had no weapons of his own, save a few hand grenades, so I gave him the Sig Saur I stole from one of the bandits. Lastly, after much arguing, we decided to try to get Vaklav in the posse. I had always known the man as a spineless coward, but it turns out he too was armed and was once a member of a hunters lodge in Slovakia before he became an anarchist.

However, my plan was put to a halt once the police arrived. Me and several other bystanders where relentlessly questioned while the injured were taken to the clinic, others were taken to the hospital. The body of the shoeshine boy was carted away to the morgue. By six in the morning, the yard was empty and everybody went home. I managed to smuggle the pistols and my violin to my flat, and hid them as I waited till nightfall. As I began to exercise vigorously, I put the war plan into action. I was prepared to die, this time by the sword rather than by the bottle like a gluttonous coward. By nightfall, I put on my overcoat and the three guns in my pockets and met the posse at the rendezvous near the lumberyard. As I walked down the empty street, I stopped and lit a cigarette, knowing it would be my last.

V

"Vaklav!" I shouted, pounding on his door. "Vaklav open up!"

It didn't take long to get a response, Vaklav finally answered, sluggishly peeping through the door crack in his underwear. He looked like he had been drinking, and heavily. He looked ahead of me to see two other men from the party who had joined the fight; the trombonist and the bartender had taken up arms.

"What do you want?" he said pathetically.

"We're going after the bastards who killed the shoeshine boy." I said. "And you said for as long as I remember how you wanted to fight but would never stand up for yourself. Dolf has bullied you for years and I'm not going to let him get away with murder, neither should you."

With that statement, Vaklav was fully awake with excitement and fear. "Are you mad? That would be suicide! Listen, Franz, I hate Dolf as much as the next guy, and I would give anything to see him suffer. But it's suicide!"

"Suicide or not," the bartender said. "I'm not letting those bastards terrorize me or anybody in this neighborhood again. You yourself where once a fighter, weren't you?"

"I was a hunter and a damn good marksman, I was even a bantamweight boxer when I was in university!" Vaklav said. Looking at the frail, bespectacled man I would have never guessed he was. And now he was showing his true colors.

"Then stand up for yourself, man!" I said. "If you were once such an athlete, then why are you so weak? Think about the glory days before you were such a pushover, you hunted wild game, you lived in mud and lived for the moment by the sword! Don't you want that again?"

"Yes!" Vaklav said, starting to tear up. "I'd give anything to be a huntsman again!"

"Well now's your chance!" The bartender said. "Hell, maybe if you survive this battle you can go back to those days. Now are you with us or not?"

"I am."

"Are you armed?" the trombonist asked.

"I have a Kalashnikov and a silencer."

With that, we had a formidable posse. Vaklav quickly changed into a set of black fatigues and boots, loaded two magazines and we all piled into a van parked outside the flat. While the bartender drove, three of us sat in the back. For what seemed like hours, we drove towards the end of town, far from civilization but close enough to the main road. Everybody knew where this stretch of road led, right towards the old factories and the lumber yard, all of which were either abandoned or scarcely in use. The land surrounding was ashen and bleached from all the smog from the copper mine, and yearly this would blow into town and cause acid rain in the summer.

This is where Moshe and the other gangsters conducted business. One of the factories which had burned down was once used to make moonshine until a still exploded. We were heading toward their main hideout and central area of business, which was the lumber yard. While the place was not heavily guarded, it was a still a suicide mission. Only the mill was guarded whenever the yard was in use, and it was said that there were two guard dogs on the premises. The bartender was prepared for this, as he had some poisoned meat in a can.

Once we reached the mill, we blackened our faces with shoe polish to make ourselves as inconspicuous as possible, and on my command, we drew our arms and snuck in the back. Quietly, we marched single file into the ruins of the lumber yard, hidden behind the piles of rotting plywood. The bartender began throwing chunks of poisoned beef in every possible direction, but there were no dogs whatsoever. In the back of the lumberyard was the old sawmill where Moshe, Dolf and their cronies set up shop. We might have been out numbered, but that didn't matter. If we could at least get to Moshe before his gang of thugs took one or all of us out, it wouldn't matter.

Using a piece of mirror to peer around the corner, we found that the entrance was guarded by two armed men. Vaklav took the first shot, since he was the only one who had a silencer on his rifle. With no effort, he climbed on top of the wood pile where we hid, aimed and fired two shots. Both guards didn't know what hit them.

With the guards out, now we just needed to get everybody out in the open. The trombonist, who was a grenadier in the army, had a few explosives prepared for such an occasion, and took out a hand grenade. Pulling the pin, he threw it towards the door and ordered us to get down. There was a deafening bang and soon there came a scuffling of feet and the shouts of disoriented men.

"Who's out there?" Moshe shouted, he was armed with a rifle, but before he could get a response, there was another blast from a shotgun as the bartender blew our cover and ran in to the fray, firing at random. He had a look in his eyes like a man who had shellshock, and the action had set off a spark in him. We couldn't tell if he had shot anybody yet, but there were screams as one of the goons was hit with a blast of deer ammo, splattering his flesh across the lumber yard. The bartender had only loaded his shotgun with two shots and didn't even stop to reload, he ran out like a mad Norseman and began bludgeoning those who crossed his path with the butt of his gun.

Just then, we had charged into the fray. Vaklav began to spray the goons with automatic fire, and soon the silencer began to turn red hot from the barrage of bullets. I couldn't see if he had wounded anybody, but as I charged after Moshe who ran back into the mill, I heard a blast of another shotgun go off. Dolf came charging into the spray of bullets, but was limping due to a shot he had taken in the calf, and the recoil from his shotgun knocked him on his ass. Vaklav, seeing his opportunity to take back the years of abuse from this man, ran toward him and blew Dolf's brains to kingdom come.

"Deus Vult!" Vaklav cried. It occurred to me then he was no longer a Marxist. But just as the man was relishing in victory, he screamed again as he doubled over, blood was pooling around the back of his shirt where a bullet hit his spine. Even if he survived, he would never be able to walk again. I came out from where I was hiding and managed to get into the mill, hell bent on finding Moshe.

I drew my weapon, looking around the bleak mill. I knew Moshe was there, hiding like a coward or luring me into a trap. And I was right, out of nowhere I felt a tremendous pain pierce my bicep. I had been shot and the shock caused me to drop my weapon. I was hit again, and felt the second shot hit me in the gut. Blood was drenching my shirt and pants, but I was determined to ignore it as I reached for my pistol. Another shot missed me by a millimeter, and just then there was a click. Moshe was standing there in plain sight, right in the light this time and in the line of fire. His gun had jammed. Moshe stood there grunting and swearing, and my vision was starting to blur. My ears were flooding with the sounds of screams and gunfire but part of me still wanted to fight. I crawled on the oil stained floor, and tried my damndest to pick up my revolver, but there was a blast from a gun in the mill. There was a gasp, but I barely heard anything else as ears started to ring. Everything went completely hazy as I collapsed to the ground.

This was it, I thought. Now I was really dead and about to meet my maker.

Epilogue

I didn't die that night.

It turns out I wasn't being lifted into the halls of Valhalla and offered a beer by Wotan, I was in a hospital bed wrapped in bandages. The Valkyrie was a nurse shoving a needle in my arm full of morphine as I lay in agony. They had taken out at three bullets from both my arm and my gut, one nearly blew my stomach to kingdom come. That would have been it, but I'm still alive and by God I can still eat and drink.

It also turns out Moshe never survived the battle. I wasn't the man who fired the shot that killed him, the trombonist got him but died in battle, he was shot by one of the thugs as he tried to get me to safety. Only the bartender and I survived, he bought me into the hospital. He never checked himself in, though and later died when his untreated wounds went gangrene. Lucky for me, nobody knew about the nature of my war with him, so the police never bought me into question. Crime in Skid Row is unknown to the outside world, the government may as well have swept the worst of the worst under the rug. After some time to recover, I took a taxi back to my flat where Ms. Krovar made me dinner like always. My violin was under my bed neatly packed away in the case and my father's revolver was in its safe next to it. I was waiting for the next week for some kind of retaliation, but nobody came looking for me. Business in Skid Row went along as it always had, one dead scumbag didn't matter, even if it was somebody well known as Moshe or Dolf. I was free to just bum around town without notice.

Eventually, I decided that things needed to change. A few bullets in my carcass was enough to wake me up. For the first time in years, my mind is made up; I decided that I no longer wanted to be miserable, lonely or apathetic. I want to play my damn violin, and more importantly, I want more than ever to be the musical god I was before. I have to get out of Skid Row. I always thought I would sink in the mud of this neighborhood, but now I don't want to. I packed up what I have left and decided to spend the night with Ms. Krovar, perhaps have a last drink at the pub for old time's sake. I'm not going to miss anybody there, so no hard good-byes are needed.

First thing in the morning, I'll take the metro to Prague, somewhere in Town Square just to see the hustling and bustling of the crowd. I'm going to stay with my brother Klaus for about a week, then I'm going to see if I can get a spot on the radio. I might play something like Bach's Chaconne or something from his Third Partita. I wanted to head to Berlin to meet with my old colleague from the Philharmonic, but Klaus dissuaded me. Some socialist-extremists have been causing trouble, and word has it that a man with a little moustache has been the mastermind behind riots and demonstrations. I'm not very well-read on politics, but rumor has it that the Great War has something to do with the unrest in Germany, something with the Treaty of Versailles and the German Surrender, or so I read in the paper.

One Great War and a war of my own is enough for a lifetime, so I think I'll get out of Europe for a while and head to America. Before I go back to Chicago like I always planned,

I think I'll stop in Florida to get some of that sunshine I've

been craving, something to heal my wounds and bring back my

natural color I lost while languishing in Skid Row. While in

Florida, I'll spend some time on the beach, then I'm going to

peruse the music in Chicago. In fact, I might even immigrate

there and become a citizen. I had plans long ago to have a flat

in the city, and now I might be able to do that again, and

someday I'm going to have Klaus and his wife and child move

in with me. We might even get my sister, Katya to join us.

From what Klaus told me she divorced her husband and lives

in a garret in New Town, and reuniting with her family should

be good for her sanity.

With that, I say good bye to this god forsaken

neighborhood, Skid Row, and every scumbag and lowlife that

live here. I won't miss it one bit!

www.ingramcontent.com/pod-product-compliance
Lightning Source LLC
Chambersburg PA
CBHW031130210626
46816CB00015B/1382